A GRIFFIN IN HER DESK

Zee Ann Poerio & James R. Clifford
Illustrated by Monica Getty

A Griffin In Her Desk is a magical excursion from the classroom into the realm of mythical monsters, Greek gods and fabulous treasures. Congratulations to James Clifford and Zee Ann Poerio for conjuring up an engaging children's story based on Greek mythology and ancient coins. I hope that more volumes in this ancient coin series will be forthcoming.

Virginia Barrett, National Committee for Latin & Greek

Your book is a delight. It's a really fresh and creative way to introduce kids to Classics through ancient coins. This is an exciting approach to bringing numismatics and classics to life for children in elementary school.

Scott Rottinghaus, MD
Classics Major
Governor, American Numismatic Association

Mrs. Moneta is the teacher we all dream of having! She makes the classics, ancient history, Greek mythology, and reading fun and educational, with her own magical twist. You and your child will love this book, and find yourselves wanting to learn and read more about the world that is introduced to us by Mrs. Moneta.

Kerry K. Wetterstrom, Editor/Publisher – The Celator

I loved reading "A Griffin In Her Desk." What a fun story and truly wonderful way to bring ancient history, mythology, and numismatics to life! I especially enjoyed the emphasis on language and your efforts to include a manageable amount of new Latin vocabulary that was effectively scattered (and repeated) throughout the story. I think you have succeeded in making ancient history and numismatics fun and exciting to a younger audience. I can only say that I am already looking forward to what future adventures will come with Mrs. Moneta and her class!

Elizabeth Hahn, Librarian, American Numismatic Society

A Griffin In Her Desk is a great way to introduce children to ancient coins and an easy to read story. It holds your interest to the end.

Richard Gaetano, Retired History Teacher
Pennsylvania Association of Numismatists,
Charter Member

The Mrs. Moneta series opens new vistas for today's young students and leads them to the Classics in a gentle but exciting way. It's what we have needed for far too long.

Wayne Sayles, Numismatist
Executive Director, Ancient Coin Collectors Guild

Photo courtesy of Classical Numismatics Group, Inc.
www.cngcoins.com

ISBN: 1-4392-5572-5
ISBN-13: 9781439255728

Visit www.mrsmoneta.com to order additional copies.

A Word from the Authors

"An ancient coin held in the hand can transport the mind to another land. Through this tiny piece of history, children learn and they remember."

– Zee Ann Poerio & James R. Clifford

The idea for the Mrs. Moneta Book Series was inspired by our lifelong interests in classical ancient history, numismatics, and the desire to share our passions with kids of all ages. We strongly feel that studying the ancient world can help all of us better understand the world we live in today.

Nothing sparks the imagination of a child's mind more than a tangible link to the past. Children are in awe when they learn that ancient civilizations used coins just as we use them today. A child makes a connection to these coins and discovers the similarities. They are motivated to investigate more, and then they wonder. Who owned these tiny pieces of history? What were they used for? Would a child in ancient times save his money to buy a toy like I do today? Through this tiny piece of history, held in the palms of their hands, children learn and they remember.

We hope to provide that tangible link by making available a replica of an ancient coin to coordinate with each book in the series. Our goal is to make ancient history and numismatics fun and exciting. Beginning with the first book in our series, *A Griffin In Her Desk,* we explore mythological creatures that were minted on ancient Greek coins. Become part of this learning adventure as Mrs. Moneta introduces a friendly griffin and other wonders of classical Greek mythology.

We hope you enjoy the book as much as we have enjoyed the process of writing it. Together, we can continue the lifelong quest of learning as we allow our imaginations to carry us away to ancient worlds.

For my parents who introduced me to the magic of books, so now I can pass that passion on to my own children-Alex, Regan, and Lindsay.

–Jamie

To my husband, Jim, my sons, Tony and Dom, my parents, my siblings, my friends, and my students for inspiring my interest in numismatics and Classics and for the support they have given me so that I can share what I have learned with others.

–Zee

Chapters

WELCOME BACK!

Chapter I

NEW TEACHER /NEW STUDENT

Ivan groaned as the ringing of the 8:15 morning bell officially started the new school year. He was the "new kid," and he was not looking forward to the first day of school.

But at least he knew where his classroom was because Sid, a boy in the other third grade class, introduced himself on the bus and told him that Ivan's class was the third door on the left past the office.

Ivan trudged behind the students who raced down the hallway expecting to be greeted by the usual third grade teacher, Mr. Littleville.

Everyone loved Mr. Littleville. He was like a kid himself and made class F-U-N. Instead, Mr. Totle, the principal, stood outside the classroom door along with a tall lady with long, dark hair that was pulled back and arranged in a fancy cluster of curls on the top of her head.

"Okay, class," Principal Totle said as the students streamed past. "Please take a seat. I have an announcement to make."

The kids hurriedly sat at any available desk while looking anxiously between Principal Totle and the tall, strange lady. Ivan trailed behind the other students and nervously entered Room 206.

"You must be Ivan Capita. Welcome to Colorado Springs. Have a seat right here." Mr. Totle pointed. "Oh, and please remove your hat."

Ivan shrank into the desk and sighed as he reluctantly removed his baseball cap. "Here we go again. New kid, new school. Why did Dad have to take a sabbatical this year? I was just getting used to East Elementary," Ivan thought to himself.

Ivan had enjoyed his many visits to Miami University of Ohio where his dad was a visiting professor in the English Department. Now, once again, he had to adjust to a new school for the sake of his dad's writing career.

Ivan felt a finger poke him right between his shoulder blades followed by, "Hey, I'm Rudy. Do you like football? Are you any good? Do you want to be on my team at recess? Are you related to Ivan the Terrible?"

Ivan turned around and blurted, "Yes, yes, yes, no." Then he turned back to face the front of the room.

"Ivan, you are not the only new face this year," Principal Totle began. "I know everyone expected Mr. Littleville to be the teacher this year, but over the summer he decided to retire."

The class groaned, but immediately stopped when Principal Totle raised his hand. "However, I am pleased to introduce your new teacher—Mrs. Moneta."

Mrs. Moneta gave the class a smile and waved to everyone. "Salvete, omnes," (*sahl-WAY-tay AHM-nays*) she said with a peculiar accent. Then she wrote s-a-l-v-e-t-e o-m-n-e-s on the board and pointed to it. "That's Latin for 'Hello, everyone!'"

"Hello," the class replied, a bit confused.

"Maybe this won't be so bad," thought Ivan. At least having a new teacher would take some of the pressure off him, especially since she seemed to have some weird obsession with Latin, which he had heard was a dead language.

Principal Totle continued, "We are very lucky to have Mrs. Moneta join our school. She has lived and traveled to many faraway places like Rome and Greece and she knows people from all over the world. I think it's going to be an interesting school year and I wish everyone good luck, or as Mrs. Moneta might say, 'Bonam Fortunam' (*BOE-nahm for-TOO-nahm).*"

Mrs. Moneta nodded appreciatively as Principal Totle left the room.

The class stared at the new teacher with curiosity. Mrs. Moneta was dressed in flowing layers of black with a scarf draped around her shoulders.

"I like your scarf, Mrs. Moneta. It's pretty," Norma said from the back of the classroom.

"Gratias (GRA-tee-ahs). That's Latin for 'Thank you,'" replied Mrs. Moneta as she glided to the center of the classroom. She spoke very quickly with a happy, but firm tone. "I am very pleased to be your teacher this year. I know everyone is familiar with the usual school rules, which are posted on the wall."

Ivan glanced over and read the rules to himself.

1) Raise your hand if you have a question.
2) Always do your best work.
3) Respect others.

"Not very original," smirked Ivan.

"Did you have a question about the rules, Ivan?" Mrs. Moneta asked.

OFF
LIMITS

"Ummmm . . . no, Mrs. Moneta," Ivan replied with embarrassment.

"I didn't think so. Then we will skip all of those, but I do have one additional rule that we must all follow."

Ivan watched as she added to the list on the wall in very neat cursive—Rule Number 4.

No student is allowed to look inside the teacher's desk.

She continued, "In particular, the right hand drawer of my desk. It is completely off-limits. Noli tangere. (NOHL-ee TAHN-ge-ray) That's Latin for 'Don't touch.'"

"Oh, I sense a challenge," thought Ivan. This sounded not only mysterious, but forbidden, and for Ivan that was a green light for trouble.

Ivan remembered his second grade teacher, Mrs. Valenti. Her desk was magical. She had an endless supply store of stickers, bookmarks, sticky notes, stopwatches, puzzles, card games, and extra-large paper clips. Ivan's favorite drawer was the snack drawer. After school, he had a late bus, and Mrs. Valenti would always have a tasty snack to share with him.

The memory of her private stash of red licorice and chocolate chip cookies was making Ivan's mouth water and it made him wonder, "Is it time for lunch yet?"

Mrs. Moneta's dramatic voice called Ivan back to reality. "Now, I am sure you have always been aware that students are not permitted in the teacher's desk. To be safe, I asked Mr. Peterson, our janitor, to install a special lock on the right hand drawer." She then held up a small metal key. "So, just be patient. I will reveal the contents of the drawer perhaps after we have settled in next week." Then she hooked the key on her keychain with a bunch of others.

The class moaned because as far as they were concerned, next week might have been a billion, trillion, gazillion years away.

Ivan, who had been voted Most Curious Second Grader at his school last year, was exceptionally interested in the mystery. He raised his hand. "Mrs. Moneta, can you at least give us a little hint what is in there?"

This question triggered a buzz of energy around the classroom but before anyone else could release a spark, Mrs. Moneta doused it. "There won't be any discussion about it. I do not want to send someone to Principal Totle's office for breaking the rules on my first day."

Her answer only fueled Ivan's imagination. What could be in there? A tasty treat? Or maybe it's all the stuff she takes from kids who are playing with things instead of paying attention during class.

Ivan remembered that Mr. Holden from East Elementary always took their "toys and trinkets" as he'd call them. He'd lock them in the bottom drawer of his file cabinet and wouldn't give them back until the last day of school or until they brought in a note from a parent.

But Mrs. Moneta didn't seem like the type to do that. Maybe she keeps souvenirs from her trips in the desk drawer? Or better yet, maybe it was some kind of a test to see if the class would try to look inside?

"Isn't that how it always goes?" Ivan reflected. Someone tells you, "No" and then it becomes the one thing you want to do the most.

The whole day the class wondered what could be inside Mrs. Moneta's desk! It was a Pandora's Box waiting to be opened and the students were just like Pandora. They wanted to see exactly what was inside.

And every chance they could get, the students tried to sneak a peak in Mrs. Moneta's desk.

Ivan especially kept careful watch and vowed to his new classmates that he would discover what the big secret was. After all, that would gain him instant popularity.

So Ivan patiently waited for any chance he could get when Mrs. Moneta unlocked the drawer. Sometimes it was open during a change of class, or a group activity. Any distraction whatsoever, and he would take the opportunity to try and peek inside.

On Wednesday, Ivan thought he caught a glimpse of a white cloth and broken eyeglasses, and then on Thursday he even thought he saw something move! But by Friday, all Ivan could tell his classmates was that the inside of the drawer was the same light oak wood as the outside of the desk.

The class was hardly impressed with his detective work and after no luck, and not wishing to get into trouble with Mrs. Moneta, Ivan decided to give up his quest.

Just before the final dismissal bell rang at 2:30 P.M., Mrs. Moneta asked Ivan to take an envelope to the office. Ivan approached the desk and out of the corner of his eye, he saw something very interesting written in Mrs. Moneta's lesson plan book.

Release the griffin on Monday.

Finally! A clue! Ivan was glad that the weekend had arrived, but he couldn't wait until Monday. Maybe that would be the day he would finally find out what was inside of Mrs. Moneta's desk!

A griffin! What could that be? Was it some kind of a small monster?

He could hardly wait to rush home and ask his dad, "What in the world is a griffin?

Chapter II

THE BIG SURPRISE

Ivan was the first at the door after gym class on Monday morning. He turned the doorknob to the classroom but it was locked. One by one his classmates arrived and lined up behind the locked door. They could see the lights were were on, and they knew Mrs. Moneta was in there.

Ivan could hardly contain himself. The anticipation was almost too much to stand! He had a pretty good idea this was about the surprise hidden in Mrs. Moneta's desk and he wanted to tell the class, but he decided he would show them how brilliant he was once they were all inside the room.

Finally, after what seemed like forever, the door slowly opened. Mrs. Moneta motioned for everyone to enter and the class rushed in quickly sitting at their desks.

"So does anyone have a guess about what I have locked inside my desk?" Mrs. Moneta asked.

The class shook their heads.

"Does it begin with a G?" Ivan called out.

"Please refer to rule number one, Mr. Capita."

"Rule number one," everyone sang and pointed to the list of rules on the wall. After that, everyone raised a hand before asking or answering any more questions.

Mrs. Moneta continued, "How do you know it Begins with a 'G,' Ivan?"

"Oh, I have this talent." Ivan grinned. "It's called being very observant, and I just happened to observe something written in your plan book on Friday when you called me to your desk."

"You are super-sleuthy, Ivan," Rudy said under his breath.

"Okay, please continue, Mr. Capita. What do you think is inside the desk?"

"I think you have a griffin in your desk, Mrs. Moneta."

"A what?" Regan called out.

"A griffin. According to my dad, it's a mythological creature."

Mrs. Moneta smiled. "That's excellent, Ivan. You are correct. Mythological means a myth or legend dealing with gods or heroes or in the case of the griffin, an animal. A griffin is a mythological animal that has the head and wings of an eagle but the body of a lion."

"Wow! That's awesome! I might try drawing one of those in my sketchbook," shouted Josette. "Does a griffin have any special powers?"

"Well, griffins are powerful creatures because they represent both an eagle who is the king of the sky and a lion who is the king of beasts. Griffins were considered sacred because they drew chariots for Zeus and they were also responsible for protecting his gold."

"Hey, I have a dog named Zeus," Quinn bragged.

Alex raised her hand. "Mrs. Moneta, who is Zeus?"

"Zeus was a Greek god. He lived with the other gods on Mount Olympus, but Zeus was the king of all of them. He ruled the sky and even created thunder and lightning."

"And you have a half lion, eagle . . . whatchamacallit animal inside your desk?" Regan asked in disbelief.

"A griffin, and yes, I do."

"Hey! That's what I must have seen moving," Ivan blurted out. "It was the griffin."

Mrs. Moneta gave Ivan a warning stare causing him to slink down in his desk chair. She walked behind her desk and unlocked the drawer with the key Mr. Peterson gave her.

This is it! The moment everyone had been waiting for! They were going to see an actual griffin.

Ivan whispered to Alex "Hey, maybe if we're lucky Mrs. Moneta might let us take turns taking the griffin home as a pet for a night or two. You know, we did that with a hamster at my old school."

The students in the first row started leaning forward causing the students sitting in the back to call out, "Hey, we can't see!" and, "Mrs. Moneta, they're standing up."

Mrs. Moneta held up a hand. "I won't open the drawer until everyone stops talking and sits in their seats properly."

The class settled back and watched as Mrs. Moneta reached in the drawer, lifted out a wooden box and then carefully placed it on the center of her desk.

"If there's a real live griffin inside that little box, it must be really tiny," Alex commented.

"Hey, maybe it will fly out like an eagle," Regan replied. "You know just like one of those silly surprise springs that pops out of a can when you aren't expecting it."

"Or it could charge forward with a giant roar like a lion," Rudy added.

The class fell silent and watched as Mrs. Moneta slowly flipped a small latch, and removed what looked like a velvet-lined tray. She then opened a plastic case and placed its contents on the tray's soft, black fabric.

Mrs. Moneta walked up to the first row of desks and handed the tray to Ivan along with a magnifying glass.

Ivan stared down for a second then whined in disappointment, "What! This is just some old coin! What happened to the griffin? Where did he go?"

"He is right in front of you." Mrs. Moneta answered. "Use the magnifying glass. Ecce. (EH-kay) That's Latin for 'Look!'"

Ivan leaned over the tray and stared through the magnifying glass at the tiny coin. "That's cool!" Sure enough, on that old silver coin was an animal that had a body of a lion and the wings of an eagle.

The class passed around the griffin coin while Mrs. Moneta explained, "What you see on the obverse, or front of the coin, is the griffin. This is a Greek coin called a drachm (*dram)*. When you flip the coin over, on the reverse is a kantharos (*KAN-ther-uhs*) with an inscription."

"Hey, that kan-tha-whatever-thing looks like a trophy I won in baseball last year," boasted Ivan.

Α
ΙΡΟΜ

"It does look a bit like a trophy but a Kantharos is a type of Greek pottery that was used for drinking," Mrs. Moneta corrected Ivan. "Very much like the way we use cups today. The coin you are looking at was minted in the 4th century BC, so it is almost 2,500 years old."

"Hey," Ivan chuckled. "That's even older than my dad."

"Wait, you said 'minting coins,' Mrs. Moneta. Did they have flavors like peppermint or spearmint?" asked Regan.

The rest of the class wasn't quite sure what minting meant either.

"Not exactly," Mrs. Moneta explained. "Minting means to produce or make money by stamping the metal. That's how coins are made or minted. They all started as small pieces of metal that were heated and then dies or special metal molds with carved images were stamped onto the metal with a hammer. That's why some of them aren't perfectly centered. Today, machines are used to mint coins."

"This coin was minted at a place called Abdera in an ancient country known as Thrace. Today, Thrace is a region in southeast Europe which is now part of southern Bulgaria, northeastern Greece and Turkey. Can anyone find Europe on our map?"

Quinn raised his hand. Mrs. Moneta gave him a nod. He walked over to the classroom map, pointed to the exact spot, and took a bow.

Everyone laughed.

"Bene!" (BEN-ay) Mrs. Moneta said in Latin. "That's Latin for 'Good.' According to legends, Abdera was founded by Hercules who was the son of Zeus."

"This coin is incredible," said Josette. "Are there other coins that have weird animals on them?"

"Yes, there are and that is our lesson plan for today. I am going to show you ancient coins with mythological creatures on them and we'll get to learn a little bit of ancient history that relates to the coins."

Mrs. Moneta looked at her watch. "But, the morning has flown by. It's already time for lunch and recess."

"Aaaaw," the class groaned because they wanted to hear more.

Mrs. Moneta gathered the velvet lined box, magnifier, and the griffin coin.

"Oh, boy, just when it was getting good," said Josette. "I wish we could hear more about griffins."

"Me, too," replied Alex.

Mrs. Moneta was happy to see her students so enthusiastic. "If you're really interested, after you finish your lunch, anyone who wants to hear more about griffins and other mythological creatures can meet me over at that lovely fountain in the playground garden. However, this is not a requirement. There are no extra credit points either. This is just if you want to learn more."

The children grabbed their lunch boxes or their lunch money for the cafeteria and lined up behind Mrs. Moneta to lead them down to the cafeteria.

There was a murmur of comments. "You know, I think I am going to the fountain instead of jumping rope today," Josette said to Alex.

"Me, too" replied Alex.

"What about you, Regan?"

"Well, if you two are going, I don't want to jump rope by myself, so count me in."

Rudy poked Ivan between the shoulder blades, "Are you going to meet at the fountain after lunch?"

"I'll think about it, if you get your pointy finger out of my back!" Ivan said.

One by one the children left the classroom with their lunch boxes.

Chapter III

LUNCH BREAK

The class walked single-file down the stairs to the cafeteria. The students who packed their lunches sat at the table first while those that bought their lunches filled in the empty seats after picking up their food from the cafeteria line.

Mrs. Moneta's class sat on the right side of the table and Mr. Carpathian's class sat opposite them.

"Dang! I knew I shouldn't have brought my lunch. The spaghetti looks good today," said Sid from Mr. Carpathian's class as he checked out Ivan's tray.

"Yeah, it's not bad," Ivan said while twisting a big fork into the plate of spaghetti. "And the salad even has cheese on it." He twirled the fork a few times and then shoved an enormous pile of spaghetti into his mouth.

"Oh, no!" Ivan cried out as a giant saucy meatball fell from his fork and landed on the front of his pants causing a large red splat. "RATS! I hate when that happens. This fork is terrible, and now my parents will know that I didn't put a napkin on my lap!"

Ivan looked around to make sure the lunch monitor wasn't watching him and then he kicked the meatball underneath the table toward Sid's feet.

Ivan then asked Sid, "What did you do in Carpathian's class this morning?"

"Nothing," replied Sid as he slowly tried pushing the meatball back into Ivan's floor space with his foot. "Except he taught us how to spell Mississippi with one I."

"What do you mean you learned how to spell Mississippi with one I?" Ivan said in a loud disbelieving voice after he blocked the meatball from crossing into his zone. "That's not possible."

"Yes, it is," Sid replied.

Sid winked and elbowed a classmate sitting next to him who passed the elbow action down the line so everyone stopped eating and began listening to Sid and Ivan's debate.

"Okay. Prove it then," challenged Ivan.

Sid looked down the table and nodded. Mr. Carpathian's entire class stood up, covered their left eye with the palm of their left hand and chanted, "m-I-s-s-I-s-s-I-p-p-I."

Then Mr. Carpathian's class all sat down on cue and started laughing at their trick.

Ivan threw up his hands. "You guys are ridiculous, I knew it was joke!"

Still laughing, Sid asked Ivan, "A bunch of the other guys and me are playing soccer at recess. Wanna play?"

"You mean 'the other guys and I,'" interrupted Ed.

"Who are you? The Grammar Patrol? It's lunch, aren't you off duty?" Sid barked at Ed. "So, Ivan, are you going to play soccer at recess with us? We'll let you play even though you can't spell as well as we can! Did you get that, Ed? I said, 'as well as we can.'"

Ed nodded.

Ivan hesitated then told Sid, "Nah, I was thinking about meeting some of the kids at the Garden Fountain today. Mrs. Moneta said she'd meet us there if we wanted to hear more about the ancient coins that she showed us during class."

"Coins? You'd rather hear about some stupid old coins than play soccer. What are you crazy or something?"

Ivan shrugged. "Well, they're kind of neat. She showed us one with a weird-looking creature on it called a griffin."

"A what? What's a griffin?"

"It's an animal that has a body of a lion and the wings of an eagle, and it flies around Mount Olympus protecting Zeus' gold."

"Aw, c'mon, Ivan," begged Sid. "I think you'd be a pretty good striker. You might even make a decent goalie judging from the way you blocked that meatball underneath the table. We need you to play."

Ivan hesitated for a second but he really wanted to get another look at that weird-looking creature and hear what else Mrs. Moneta had to say. He could always play soccer another day.

"Nah, you guys can play without me. I'm going to listen to Moneta's story at the fountain. She tells a pretty good story, and it's so hot today. Maybe we'll get to splash around in the water when she's not looking."

Sid shrugged. "Whatever. Have fun flying around Mount Olympus! And don't forget to pick up that meatball under your seat, the lunch monitors have more eyes than Mississippi!

Chapter IV

THE FOUNTAIN

Mrs. Moneta walked out of school through the playground and over to the Garden Fountain. She smiled as she counted the group of children who had gathered there. Everyone from her class was waiting.

She spotted Ivan tossing a handful of pennies into the fountain splashing three different children.

"Hey, cut that out!" Josette yelled.

"Aw, you got splashed, what's the big deal?" Ivan replied.

Mrs. Moneta walked up behind the class. "Ivan, if you are going to toss coins into the ancient well for the favors of the water gods, that's not the way to do it."

Everyone turned and saw Mrs. Moneta standing behind them.

Ivan raised an eyebrow. "Huh?"

Mrs. Moneta continued, "I said the water gods will smile kindly upon you and grant your requests only if you make a worthy votive offering and show respect."

Mrs. Moneta pulled the griffin coin from her pocket and held it up in front of everyone. Then she tossed it up into the air.

The children watched in disbelief and shock as the coin rose then fell into the fountain quickly sinking to the bottom.

"Mrs. Moneta! Your griffin!" Ivan cried out.

Mrs. Moneta pointed to the fountain. "Ecce! (EH-kay) Look."

The children leaned over the fountain to see if they could spot where the griffin coin had come to rest. As they searched for the coin they noticed the water started to ripple and small bubbles began to surface where the coin had landed. In the water they saw the distorted reflection of the school building, and the hill where children sat to watch the soccer game.

The water calmed and they saw the reflection of an animal flying in the sky above them.

"Hey, that looks like a griffin," exclaimed Ivan.

The students quickly looked up, but the only things they saw were fluffy white clouds in the sky.

The students turned back toward the fountain, and Mrs. Moneta dipped her finger in the water. "Observe. I am about to show you a real surprise. You will see something you have never seen before . . . pay attention . . ."

She stirred the water causing the dirt from the bottom to rise up making the water murky and gray.

Faster and faster the water was churned. Then the most astonishing thing happened, as the dirt swirled around in the fountain the water turned a brilliant red . . . then orange, yellow, green, blue, indigo, and violet.

"Hey, those are the colors of a rainbow," called out Alex.

Then the students felt a sudden draw almost like a magnetic tug or the feeling of a current pulling a boat. But there was no boat and they weren't even in the water.

Their eyes were fixated on the moving rainbow-colored water and the spinning particles kicked up from the bottom of the fountain.

They tried to make out the shapes that were forming in the water clouds of dirt, and the class felt themselves being drawn closer and closer.

"Ecce (EH-kay). Ecce. Look." Mrs. Moneta chanted.

They continued to stare down at the reflections in the murky water.

Mrs. Moneta continued, "Where is the school and the playground? Everything is changing or disappearing… and now even the fountain itself."

Chapter V

GRYPHON AND MOUNT OLYMPUS

Mrs. Moneta raised her hand to her forehead to shade the bright sunlight from her eyes. "What's that far into the distance. Do you see that majestic mountain and that beautiful sea?"

Alex and Regan rolled their eyes at each other. Rudy shrugged his shoulders because he wasn't sure what to make of Mrs. Moneta's odd behavior.

Ivan finally broke the class' silence. "Yeah. I see it. And it's even bigger than I imagined!"

Mrs. Moneta pointed. "Exactly, that is definitely Mount Olympus. Home of the twelve Olympians."

"You mean that is where people who play in the Olympics live?" Ivan asked.

"Not quite. That is where the twelve Greek gods and goddesses live. They are called the Olympians not because they play sports but because they live on Mount Olympus."

"What are their names?" Josette asked.

Mrs. Moneta thought for a second. “Their names? Let me see. There is: Zeus, Hera, Poseidon, Demeter, Ares, Hermes, Hephaestus, Aphrodite, Athena, Apollo, Artemis, and Hestia.”

“Those are pretty weird names,” Ivan said to Rudy. “I‘ve heard the name, Apollo, but that was in science class when we talked about the astronauts.”

“Yeah,” Rudy said getting ready to poke Ivan between the shoulder blades. “That was the name of a space shuttle or something I think.”

Mrs. Moneta peered off toward the mountain. “Ah ha!” she exclaimed. “There it is. Look near the base of the mountain.”

The kids stared in the direction Mrs. Moneta was pointing.

“I see it,” Ivan confirmed. “There’s an odd-looking animal guarding a pathway leading up the mountain.”

“Hey, it’s a real-life griffin!” yelled Quinn.

“And it’s just like you said, Mrs. Moneta,” Regan exclaimed loudly. “A griffin really does have the wings and a head of an eagle.”

“And it looks just like the one on the coin,” Alex pointed out.

The griffin's head turned toward the class then its giant wings spread open.

"Oh no, I think he's seen us," Alex said nervously.

With one quick motion the griffin flapped its wings and rose up into the air like a slow-moving hummingbird. It flew toward the class and landed only a few yards away.

In a strong, deep voice the griffin addressed them, "I am Gryphon. I welcome you on behalf of the gods and goddesses of Mount Olympus. I am one of Zeus' hounds. As protector of his gold, I must warn you. I shall defend his treasure against all who would seek to plunder it. You are not here to steal his treasure, are you?"

"Why, no, Gryphon," Mrs. Moneta said while slowly offering her open hand.

The class held their breath for a moment.

The beast hesitated then extended his massive claw in return, and they carefully shook.

"We have no intentions of stealing Zeus' treasure. I am Mrs. Moneta and this is my class. We are scholars in search of our own treasure—the wealth of knowledge that we can share with others. Maybe you can help us learn about Zeus' treasure and Mount Olympus?"

Gryphon spread his enormous wings and bowed. "It pleases me greatly that you have traveled so far to visit, and it would be my honor to accompany you. For there is much to learn about all that you seek."

Regan pointed up toward the top of the mountain. "Oh my gosh! Does Zeus live all the way up there?"

"Yes. Mount Olympus is Zeus' home, but he is not here right now. The twelve gods and goddesses, along with Zeus' son, Hercules, are off battling the Titans. I stayed behind to protect Zeus' gold hidden inside Mount Olympus from the forces who would desire to take it."

"But who would want to steal Zeus' gold?" asked Ivan.

Gryphon sighed loudly. "The Arimaspians."

"The-Hairy-Mass-Peas?" interjected Ivan. "I've never heard of them but I think, maybe, I had that for lunch at school once."

The whole class burst out laughing.

"Not-Hairy Mass Peas," Gryphon corrected. "Air-rih-MASS-pee-uhns."

"Arimaspians (air-rih-MASS-pee-uhns)," The class repeated.

Gryphon pointed a sharp claw towards a small river running behind Mount Olympus. "They live next to the river. They are a tribe of one-eyed creatures."

"One-eyed!" cried Regan. "Like one of those mean-looking Cyclopes."

"Yes, kind of like a Cyclops, only not as big. But they are crafty little critters who spend the majority of their time trying to steal gold. Alas, somehow they discovered Zeus and the other gods had left and they have been trying to steal his gold ever since."

"Why do they want to take other people's gold?" asked Regan.

Gryphon's wings flapped open. "I know this may sound odd, but they love to adorn their hair with it."

Ivan made a sour face. "Yuk! Even the boys?"

"Yes, even the boys. It's practically the only thing they think about."

"I guess it's a good thing Zeus left you behind to protect his gold," Mrs. Moneta replied.

"Yes. But Zeus has been gone longer than expected, and I am growing weary of fighting the Arimaspians by myself. I don't know how much longer I can keep them from the gold."

"Do they try to steal Zeus' gold every single day?" Quinn asked.

"Every day after lunch they begin scaling Mount Olympus in an attempt to breach Zeus' chamber. And they almost made it the other day before I managed to turn them back at the last moment."

Josette stepped forward. "We'll help you, Gryphon."

"Yeah, we're not afraid of any 'Hairy Peas,'" Ivan shouted to his classmates. "Are we?"

"No way!" Everyone yelled back.

Gryphon bowed. "I am indebted to you for your courage and kindness. Thank you for your help. It is most welcome."

"Gryphon," Mrs. Moneta said. "Why don't you tell us about Mount Olympus and how we can help you defend Zeus' treasure from the Arimaspians."

Gryphon's tail excitedly flipped from side-to-side. "That's an excellent idea. There is much to learn. Follow me."

They walked across the plain into a grove of olive trees and right smack in the middle of the olive trees was an enormous golden chariot.

"Holy Toledo!" Ivan exclaimed. "Are we actually going to get to ride in Zeus' golden chariot, Gryphon?"

"It will be my pleasure to give you and the class your first chariot ride into the clouds. Hold on tight!"

"Hooray!" the class yelled as they climbed into the giant golden chariot.

Chapter VI

ZEUS' GOLD

The Chariot soared to the top of Mount Olympus and Gryphon gently landed it in an open courtyard. The courtyard was adorned with colorful flowers, and tall marble statues lined the pathway leading to an enormous columned temple.

The class hopped out of the chariot followed by Mrs. Moneta and Gryphon.

"Welcome to Zeus' home," Gryphon announced.

The class stared around wide-eyed and Regan asked, "Who built this awesome place?"

"The entire palace was built by Cyclopes who were thankful to Zeus for saving them from being banished to Tartarus."

"Tartar Sauce?" Ivan said in confusion. "I thought that was used on fish sandwiches? Why would the Cyclopes be afraid of that?"

Gryphon was more confused than Ivan. "I don't know what tartar sauce is but Tartarus (*TAHR-ter-uhs*) *is* a place even lower than the underworld of Hades.

It is a place no one wants to go, and Zeus saved a group of Cyclopes from being banished there. In return, they built this palace for him."

"Is that Zeus' throne?" Mrs. Moneta asked, pointing at an enormous chair.

The class stared in awe at the black marble throne. A golden eagle sat perched on the right arm of the throne with a purple fleece covering the seat. Seven steps led up to the throne and each step was a different color of the rainbow.

"Yes," Gryphon answered. "And next to that is the throne of Zeus' wife, Queen Hera."

Three crystal steps led to the queen's throne carved of white ivory.

"Tell us more," said Rudy.

Gryphon sat back on his hind legs, raised his head, settled his feathers and began, "Zeus has two brothers and three sisters. When their father died, the brothers drew lots to divide up the world."

"What are lots?" Alex asked Gryphon.

Gryphon stared at Mrs. Moneta with a perplexed look.

"It's a game like drawing straws," answered Mrs. Moneta. "Whoever gets the shortest straw loses."

"Exactly," Gryphon continued, "So Zeus became the God of the Heavens. He is the King of the Sky, God of Rain and the Cloud Gatherer. He also wields mighty lightning bolts and can hurl them against anyone who displeases him."

"What about his two brothers?" Alex asked.

"Poseidon became the King of the Seas, and Hades was assigned Lord of the Underworld. But Zeus is the King of all Gods. He has many powers and because of that the gods have voted Zeus to be king forever. He is not afraid of anyone or anything." Gryphon paused then added, "except his wife."

Mrs. Moneta laughed and Gryphon motioned to the kids. "Follow me. I have something special to show you."

Gryphon led them around Zeus' throne past a series of gigantic columns and into Zeus' palace. The ceiling seemed a mile high. Exquisite paintings and frescos adorned the walls.

The class followed Gryphon to the back of the room over to a small opening cut into the mountain. The entrance opened up into a dark tunnel, and Gryphon began walking down a twisting passageway, deeper and deeper into Mount Olympus with the children following slowly behind, carefully stepping over bumpy rocks. Finally, they all reached a large lit chamber.

The children entered the chamber and stared, speechless. Dozens of flaming torches lit the room, revealing chests overflowing with gold and silver coins gleaming in the light.

Gryphon whispered, "This is Zeus' treasure. The treasure the Arimaspians have been trying to steal."

Gryphon walked over to a chest and picked up a silver coin. "I come down here quite often to look at Zeus' coins. They are tiny works of art. Here, look at this one."

He showed the coin to the class.

ΣΕ

The class gathered around the coin. Ivan pushed his way to the front to get a better look. "Yuk. That thing looks mean. What the heck is it?"

"It's called a Gorgon. See its grotesque tongue protruding from its mouth?"

The class nodded.

"A Gorgon has razor-sharp fangs, large pig tusks and hideous eyes," said Gryphon. "But worse than that, Gorgons have hair of living snakes."

"Gross!" exclaimed Quinn. "I guess they don't comb their hair much. Have you ever seen one?"

"Unfortunately, yes. They fight with the Titans against the gods."

Gryphon picked up another coin and passed it to Alex. "Here's a Chimera (*ki-MEER-uh*)."

"Chimera." Alex repeated squinting at the image. "What's on its back?"

"Yet another frightful monster," Gryphon answered. "The Chimera has the body and head of a lion, the tail of a snake and the head of a goat coming out of its back. It spits fire and devours anything in its path."

"That's disgusting," said Alex. "I'd stay far away from one of those."

Mrs. Moneta cleared her throat. "Gryphon, are there any coins here without monsters on them?"

"There are. Take a look at these." Gryphon handed each student a coin.

"Look—a horse with wings," said Josette.

"That's Pegasus (*PEG-uh-suhs*), the winged horse who helps the gods. Zeus trusts him especially to bring him his lightning and thunderbolts."

"Speaking of Zeus, how can we help you protect his gold?" Mrs. Moneta asked Gryphon.

Gryphon shrugged and his giant wings sank down to the floor. "I have used every tactic known to a griffin. I fear it is a lost cause." The griffin looked around the treasure-laden room in despair. "It is only a matter of time before they will be able to take the gold."

Mrs. Moneta stepped forward. "Don't give up just yet, Gryphon, because you have Mrs. Moneta's class here to help, and we won't let that happen, will we?"

"No way!" the class shouted.

Mrs. Moneta motioned for everyone to gather around. "Okay, let's brainstorm some ideas just like we do when we are trying to solve a problem in class."

The class formed a circle around Mrs. Moneta and Gryphon.

"Hey Gryphon," Ivan blurted out. "There's only one path that leads to the top of Mount Olympus. What if we roll large boulders down it as the Arimaspians come up? That would show them."

"That's a good idea, but I've tried it. They are almost as fast as Zeus' lightning bolts, and they just jump out of the way."

"Ah, pickles!" exclaimed Alex. "But what if we just put giant boulders on the path blocking their way?"

"Another excellent suggestion, but they are superior climbers and would just climb over or around the rocks with ease."

Quinn raised his hand. "Wait a minute, why don't we just fight them off? There are plenty of sticks and rocks around here."

Gryphon shook his feathered eagle's head. "The Arimaspians are small in size but what they lack in height, they make up for with tenacity. Plus, they far outnumber us. I'd rather lose Zeus' gold than see anyone get hurt."

"Gryphon's right," Mrs. Moneta said. "We have to outsmart them. We need to use their weaknesses against them, and I think I have an idea that might work. How, about if we . . ."

The kids moved closer around Mrs. Moneta as she explained her strategy. When she finished, everyone agreed that it was a great plan.

The only question was—would the Arimaspians fall for it?

Chapter VII

THE BATTLE

The class returned to Zeus' main chamber just as a deafening blare of trumpets echoed across the plains of Mount Olympus.

"That sound!" cried Gryphon. "That's their signal to advance. We're under attack."

Everyone ran out into Zeus' courtyard and looked down to the plain where a large mass of Arimaspians had assembled.

"Yeeks!" screeched Regan. "They sure are funny looking, with only one eye."

The trumpeters let out one final ear-piercing blast, and the class watched as the Arimaspians began climbing Mount Olympus.

"You're right, Gryphon," Ivan said. "Those little 'Hairy Pea' people are fast little critters. They're already halfway up Mount Olympus."

Gryphon paced back and forth with his tail flailing from side-to-side. "I don't like this one bit. Do you really think we should wait and allow them to climb up all the way into Zeus' chamber unchallenged? Are you sure that your idea will work, Mrs. Moneta?"

"Don't worry, Gryphon," Alex said. "Mrs. Moneta is pretty smart."

"Yeah, her plan will work," said Ivan followed by similar comments from the rest of the class who were all trying their best to reassure Gryphon.

Gryphon sighed. "I hope you're right because the thought of disappointing Zeus is unbearable."

Mrs. Moneta and her students watched as the Arimaspians climbed . . . and climbed . . . and climbed . . . until they were only one ledge away. One minute went by then another. The students waited without saying a word.

"Hey guys," Alex whispered breaking the eerie silence. "Check that out over there."

The class watched as a single little Arimaspian head peered over the top of the ledge. Then another one-eyed head popped up, followed by another . . . and another . . . and another.

In no time the whole group had flung themselves over the ledge into Zeus' courtyard. The little one-eyed people stood at the edge of the cliff holding tightly woven nets.

"Confident little guys," Mrs. Moneta said to Gryphon.

Gryphon moaned, "They even brought nets to carry away Zeus' gold."

The two groups stood in a straight line facing each other. An Arimaspian stepped forward and raised his hand causing all of the little one-eyed people to drop their nets.

He then bowed. "I am Acanatha, leader of the Arimaspians."

Mrs. Moneta chuckled.

"What do you find so amusing, woman?" Acanatha scowled.

Mrs. Moneta stepped forward. "That's Mrs. Moneta to you, good sir."

Acanatha took another step closer. "I repeat myself. Ah, Mrs. Moneta. What do you find so amusing?"

"Your name, good sir. I am a teacher of Latin and your name struck me as funny."

Acanatha's face turned a deep color of red. "And why is that?"

"Well, Acanatha is Acanatha comes from a word that means 'thorn.' And from what Gryphon has told us, you certainly have lived up to your name."

"That's right," Gryphon interjected. "Acanatha and his little army have been a thorn in my side for many years."

The class laughed and Acanatha pointed a small crooked finger at Gryphon. "The game is over, hound of Zeus. We have breached Zeus' chamber. It is time to give up Zeus' gold."

"Wait. Just a moment, please," Mrs. Moneta addressed Acanatha. "I have heard an amazing claim about your people."

"And what could that be?" Acanatha asked skeptically.

"I understand that Armispians are the world's greatest game players."

A look of pride shined across Acanatha's face. "Yes. We are most fond of playing games, and we are the best game-players in the world. But how do you know this?"

"We learned of your abilities from reading many books. I am a teacher and these are my students from school."

Acanatha scratched his head. "School. What is school?"

The class laughed at such a ridiculous question.

Mrs. Moneta frowned. "You don't know what school is?"

"No, we don't know what school is!" stammered Acanatha. "We don't need to know 'school' because we are the greatest game players in the world. Why would we have a need for this 'school?'"

"For one, you can learn many great skills that will help you become even better game players. That is, if you were to go to school."

Acanatha waved a hand angrily. "We are already the best. We don't need to go to school to learn anything. You are wasting our time. We came here for the gold, not to play child's games with a bunch of two-eyes. You and that beast have been defeated, and the prize for our victory is the gold. Step aside!"

"Gladly," Mrs. Moneta said, and the class parted.

The Arimaspians lined up behind their leader and began to move forward, but Mrs. Moneta stepped in front of them blocking their passage.

"But first, before you take the gold, we challenge you to play one game with us."

The Arimaspians halted their advance and Acanatha waved his hand in the air. "Get out of our way. We have no time for games today."

Quinn cried out behind Mrs. Moneta, "But I thought you were the greatest game players in the world."

"Yeah, c'mon. What are you, scared?" teased Ivan. "You can play one little game with us."

"You're not afraid of losing to a bunch of school kids. Are you?" egged Alex.

The Arimaspians looked at their leader, who suddenly appeared hesitant about letting their challenge go unmet.

Mrs. Moneta knew she had to provide the right incentive to get them to play the game or all would be lost, so she gave it her best shot.

"Acanatha, it would be an honor for our class to be in a contest with you. In fact, should you win we promise to share the story of your great victory. We will tell our entire school of your legendary powers, and we will document our defeat to the Arimaspians in our journals."

Acanatha furrowed his brow and Mrs. Moneta added, "And, if you beat us, we will also help you carry the gold all the way to your village. Right, Gryphon?"

Gryphon moaned and reluctantly nodded.

Acanatha flashed a crooked smile revealing tiny, jagged gray teeth. "We accept your challenge. We will play ONE game. One game only. We are so confident of our victory we'll even let you pick the game. So what shall it be, Mrs. Moneta?"

Mrs. Moneta rubbed her chin. "Hmm . . .How about a game of Simon Says?"

"Simon Says?" Acanatha turned back to face his companions. "We've never heard of that. What kind of a game is that? And how is it played?"

"Oh, it's very easy. We'll teach you. One person is 'IT,' or 'Simon,' in this case, and that will be me," Mrs. Moneta explained. "Everyone must do what Simon tells you do to do. For example, if I say, 'Simon says jump,' then everyone must jump. However, if I simply say 'jump,' without first saying 'Simon says,' anyone that jumps is out of the game. The last person standing wins."

"Ha!" Acanatha scoffed. "That is the easiest game I've ever heard of. We will have no trouble defeating you. We are ready to begin. Let's play."

The teams lined up and the game of Simon Says began. One by one, Mrs. Moneta's students were eliminated. And whenever one of the students lost, they quietly circled behind the Arimaspians who were so intent on winning they weren't paying attention to anything else.

The game continued until only Ivan was left standing while not a single Arimaspian had made a mistake.

"It looks as though you are clearly beaten," Acanatha laughed confidently. "I told you we were the greatest game-players ever."

"I believe you may be right," Mrs. Moneta said in a dejected tone, "but, the game is not over yet." She continued, "Simon Says, cover your eye with your left hand and count to twenty."

All the Arimaspians covered their only eye with their left hand which left them blind. They began counting, "One . . . Two . . . Three . . ."

Mrs. Moneta motioned to her class, and the students picked up all of the Arimaspians' nets.

The Arimaspians went on counting. ". . . Seventeen . . . Eighteen. . . Nineteen . . ."

Mrs. Moneta gave the signal and commanded, "Ite! (EE-tay). Go!"

The class threw the nets over the heads of the Arimaspians.

"What trickery is this?" Acanatha yelled out while flinging his arms and legs in all directions.

His protest was followed by shouts and cries from the other Arimaspians, "Ouch!" . . . and . . . "Hey, you're kicking me!" . . . and . . . "Quit it, you hit me right in the eye!"

The harder the Arimaspians tried to escape, the more entangled they became, until finally they had worn themselves out.

Mrs. Moneta's class stared down at the exhausted creatures as they lay still in a jumbled mess of arms and legs.

Gryphon flapped his wings and rose up in the air. "Your plan worked, Mrs. Moneta! We are victorious!"

"What are you going to do with us?" blubbered Acanatha.

Mrs. Moneta stood over the twisted, defeated little game players. "Zeus should be arriving any time now. But, just to make sure you don't cause any more trouble, Gryphon is going to fly you far away from Mount Olympus, to the city of Dion. From there, we will call upon Pegasus to fly you to Rome."

"Woe is me," whimpered Acanatha." I knew we should have never have played a game with a bunch of two-eyes. It's not fair. You used your school trickery."

Mrs. Moneta smiled. "That's right. Perhaps after your long walk from Rome, you can start a school and learn some valuable skills instead of spending all day playing games and trying to steal gold that doesn't belong to you."

The class held the nets tightly as Gryphon flew above the tangled Arimaspians.

"I shall return shortly," Gryphon announced as he grabbed the ends of the nets in his enormous beak. With the muddled Arimaspians in tow, he flew off toward Dion.

The students ran to the ledge and watched as Gryphon carried them farther and farther into the distance.

Chapter VIII

THE LESSON

With Gryphon away and with a little time on their hands, Mrs. Moneta decided a lesson might be in order. She led the class back to Zeus' treasure chamber.

"Okay, class, while we wait for Gryphon to return, we can review what we've learned."

The class sat in a circle around Mrs. Moneta, who picked up a few of Zeus' coins and passed them around.

The coins didn't look like pennies, nickels, or even the state quarters. Some had jagged edges and the lettering was in a strange language. The children also noticed that none of the coins had any dates.

"Has anyone ever collected coins or know anyone else who collects them?" Mrs. Moneta asked.

"Yeah, my grandfather collects silver dollars," answered Rudy.

"And my great aunt has a flowered tin with buffalo nickels in it under her bed," added Quinn.

"My brother has a bunch of Mercury Dimes – er Winged Liberty Head dimes, he calls them," Ivan boasted. "He says they are made almost completely of silver and you can't see any copper when you look at them sideways."

Not to be outdone, Josette said, "My grandfather gives me a special set of shiny new coins in a plastic case every year on my birthday."

"That is what we call a PROOF set," said Mrs. Moneta. "That means the coins were never circulated or used to buy anything. They are special and kept for collections. That's a really wonderful gift!"

"I am so impressed with how much you know about coins. It seems like everyone here knows a numismatist."

"A num-is . . . what?" the class mumbled.

Mrs. Moneta slowly pronounced the word again, "noo-MIZ-muh-tist. A numismatist is a person who studies or collects coins."

After a couple of tries, "numismatist" was rolling off the kids' tongues.

"That's pretty weird to collect money. I'd rather spend it on video games," chuckled Ivan.

"Lots of people feel that way, Ivan, but money can be used for things other than spending. Learning about money from different places and times can help you learn about other civilizations, their history, their people and culture."

Josette raised her hand. "But why do all these coins have strange-looking animals on them?"

"Many of the earliest known coins had images of mythological creatures and animals on them. But ancient coins didn't just have animals minted on them; they had many different themes. There were coins minted with great architectural works, gods and goddesses, battles, ships, comets, kings, religious symbols . . . You name it. Just about anything you can think of was probably minted on ancient coins."

Ivan jumped up. "Hey, I think I hear something. C'mon guys."

The class stood up and ran back up the tunnel into Zeus' main chamber.

Chapter IX

ZEUS RETURNS

They were greeted by Gryphon who had a big grin. "I think that should take care of them for a couple days."

The children gathered around Gryphon. "When do you think Zeus will be back?" Rudy asked.

"I'm not sure, but I know he wishes he could be here to personally thank everyone." Gryphon stopped then raised his claw and pointed toward the horizon. "Look! Out there!"

The kids turned to see giant white clouds billowing up from mountains far off in the distance.

"Uh-oh, looks like a bad storm is on its way," Alex said.

Gryphon flapped his wings and rose a few feet off the ground. "That's not a storm. It's Zeus."

The class cheered as they rushed to the entrance to watch the grand return of the King of the Gods.

In the distance billowing white clouds turned dark then lightning bolts sprang out in all directions. The wind picked up and suddenly, from the center of the clouds, a giant golden chariot appeared, pulled by four griffins.

The students huddled together near Mrs. Moneta, covering their ears from the loud blasts of thunder.

"Zeus has returned!" Gryphon announced.

The kids scattered around to make room for Zeus' chariot, which made a perfect landing in the middle of the courtyard.

Zeus stepped out of the chariot. The King of Gods wore a green wreath on top of his long, dark hair. He had a full beard that hung low off his chin and was at least ten feet tall with muscles bigger than boulders!

Zeus smiled and greeted everyone in his booming voice, "Welcome. I trust that Gryphon has treated you well."

"He's the best!" the kids shouted back to Zeus.

Gryphon walked over to Zeus and in an excited voice recounted how Mrs. Moneta's class had helped him stop the Arimaspians from stealing all of Mount Olympus' gold.

After Gryphon finished telling of their heroic efforts, Zeus laughed so loud the mountain shook.

Zeus proudly stared down at the class. "I am indebted to each of you for your bravery and clever thinking. You are always welcome atop Mount Olympus."

Mrs. Moneta bowed. "Thank you, Zeus. Our visit has been a wonderful and educational journey. Now we must return because we have math lessons scheduled for the afternoon."

The class groaned. "No, please, Mrs. Moneta! Can't we stay?"

"It just hit me like a lightning bolt!" Zeus addressed Mrs. Moneta. "I thought you looked familiar! Are you related to Juno Moneta, the protectress of funds?"

Mrs. Moneta smiled shyly and glanced back at her students, who were trying to figure out what that could possibly mean.

Mrs. Moneta winked to Zeus. "We may be distant relatives."

"I thought so. You sure did your job today! Alas, I do understand the importance of math, but before you go. . ." Zeus pulled a bag out of his chariot and sat on his throne. "I have a gift for each of you as a token of my appreciation. I present this Greek coin to each one of you as payment for your valiant efforts. Share your treasure with others by telling them the valuable lessons you've learned today."

Zeus began handing the coins out.

"Wow! This is a treasure. It's just like the coin Mrs. Moneta had locked inside her desk," exclaimed Alex.

"It is my hope that you will always remember Gryphon and your adventure on Mount Olympus."

Gryphon beamed and Ivan shouted, "Three cheers for Zeus and Gryphon!"

"HIP HIP HORRAY! HIP HIP HORRAY! HIP HIP HORRAY!"

Zeus raised his arms and the clouds surrounding Mount Olympus disappeared leaving behind a deep blue sky. Then Gryphon and Mrs. Moneta directed the students into Zeus' chariot.

Gryphon flapped his wings. "Off we go."

The chariot rose and the class waved goodbye to Zeus as they flew off Mount Olympus. Halfway down the mountain a light mist suddenly appeared and the sky began changing colors, just as the school fountain had.

Red, then orange, yellow, green, blue, indigo, and violet.

"What's happening?" Regan asked excitedly.

"A rainbow," Alex called out. "We're flying though a rainbow!"

Chapter X

BACK TO CLASS

Droplets of falling rain brought the students' attention back to looking for Mrs. Moneta's coin in the fountain. The rain dappled the reflection of the school and empty playground. The class looked around just as the sun peeked through dark rain clouds and a large rainbow filled the sky.

"Did everyone like my griffin surprise?" Mrs. Moneta asked as she recovered the coin from the fountain and dried it off with her scarf.

"Uh huh," the class muttered, still mesmerized.

"Now that was one weird recess," Regan whispered to Alex.

Alex shrugged her shoulders. "Yeah, but it sure was fun."

"All right, everyone," Mrs. Moneta announced. "Recess is over. It's time to go inside for our math lessons."

The class marched across the playground with everyone in agreement. That was ***THE BEST*** recess ever!

When Mrs. Moneta and her class reached their classroom, they found Mr. Totle waiting for them.

"Ah, Mrs. Moneta. I was looking for you and your class at recess, but I couldn't find you anywhere. Where have you been?"

"We were in the fountain courtyard having a lesson," began Mrs. Moneta.

Principal Totle smirked. "I looked there . . ."

"Well, then we went on a little field trip," Mrs. Moneta said with a smile. "We must have just missed you."

"And what were we studying about today, some new plant life?" Principal Totle inquired.

"No, we learned about griffins and Zeus," Ivan answered.

"Griffins!" Principal Totle exclaimed. "That doesn't sound botanical. I believe I remember from my studies that a griffin is a type of a mythological animal."

"That's right," Alex said. "And we even met one named Gryphon."

Principal Totle smiled. "I do say, Mrs. Moneta, you really know how to ignite your students' imagination." He looked around the class then added, "Because, of course, we all know griffins are legends, myths."

A small clinking noise interrupted the principal. He looked down, bent over, and picked up a coin that had fallen out of Ivan's pocket.

Principal Totle held up the coin. "Ivan, I'm impressed, you even have a coin with a griffin on it. Where in the world did you get it?"

"From Zeus on Mount Olympus!" Ivan replied.

Mrs. Moneta and the class burst out laughing.

"Right. . . Mount Olympus." Principal Totle laughed.

"Well, wait till next week," Mrs. Moneta said. "We are going to have a visit from Medusa. Now, she's quite a character. You should stop in to see her 'lively' hairstyle. I'll even show you how you can look at her without turning to stone."

"Awesome!" Ivan shouted without raising his hand, forgetting about rule number 3.

Principal Totle returned the griffin coin to Ivan. "Gee, I sure wish I'd had you as a teacher when I was a student, Mrs. Moneta. Well, keep up the good work. Oh, I almost forgot why I was looking for you and your class. Ivan, I heard from the lunch monitors that there was a little meatball incident at lunch."

Oh great, here it comes, thought Ivan. Detention.

Then Principal Totle said, "I know you're still new, Ivan, so I wanted to warn you that the forks are a little slippery on spaghetti days."

About the Authors

Zee Ann Poerio lives in Pittsburgh, Pennsylvania, with her husband and 2 sons. A graduate of Washington & Jefferson College, she has dual certification in Art and Elementary Education. She has been teaching for 12 years at St. Louise de Marillac School in Pittsburgh, Pennsylvania.

She received a Golden Apple Award for Excellence in Teaching from the Diocese of Pittsburgh in 2002, the Arthur Patch McKinlay Scholarship from the American Classical League in 2003, the Harlan J. Berk Award for Teacher Excellence in 2004, and the Friend of Numismatics Award in 2005 by the Ancient Coin Collector's Guild. She has been recognized by numismatic organizations for her work using ancient coins in the classroom. She is the Past Chair for the Excellence Through Classics Committee of the American Classical League and is the current Chair of the Committee for Latin in Elementary Schools. She serves as Director of Community Outreach and Special Projects for Ancient Coins for Education, Inc. and on the Education and Youth Services Task Force for the

Ancient Coin Collectors Guild. She is also a member of the American Numismatic Association and the Pennsylvania Association of Numismatists.

Zee Ann has presented at educational conferences nationwide and organized educator workshops to promote the study of ancient coins and Classics. She serves as one of two U.S. teachers on the Primary Latin Project in the U.K. She has written plays, articles, and lesson plans for educational publications and websites. See www.etclassics.org and www.ancientcoinsforeducation.org for more information. Zee Ann's passion and obsession with the ancient world comes to fruition in the Mrs. Moneta Series which she co-authored as an introduction to coins and Classics.

James R. Clifford novels include *Double Daggers, Blackbeard's Gift*, and *Ten Days to Madness*. He is also the co-author of the Mrs. Moneta Series which promotes ancient coins and Classics through children's adventure books.

His most recent book, *Double Daggers,* received excellent reviews including being listed by American Numismatic Association as one of their "books of the year for 2006," a reviewer's choice for Midwest Book Review, and was selected as feature novel by Alan Caruba, editor of BookViews and a founding member of the National Book Critics' Circle. Additionally, *Double Daggers* was an award-winning finalist in the historical fiction category for the Indie Excellence Book Awards at the 2007 New York Book Exposition.

Jamie is an avid collector of ancient coins and is a member of the American Numismatic Association, the American Numismatic Society and the Ancient Coin Collectors Guild. He lives with his wife and three daughters and works full time as a stock commodities broker in Charleston, South Carolina. More information about Jamie and his books can be found at www.jrclifford.com.